Aeppol 圖文 · 簡郁璇 譯

成爲你的森林

너의 숲이 되어줄게 | 애뽈의 숲소녀 일기

稍作休憩也很棒呢

從小，我就很喜歡《彼得潘》這部童話。不管是從大人的世界逃離，或者是保有各自的童心，幸福快樂地在夢幻島生活的情節都令我印象深刻。我一邊想像著，一邊帶著真誠的心意，畫下一張又一張的作品，並集結成《成為你的森林》。

擁有一頭烏黑長髮的少女，與她的動物朋友們一同住在綠意盎然的蓊鬱森林裡。隨著四季而變化萬千的森林色彩與自然景致，形成日常生活的風景；仰望夜空繁星時，彌足珍貴的感性也在剎那間湧現。而這名森林少女，在不受外界的拘束之下，尋找著自己喜愛的事物，過著草綠色般愜意自在、充滿清香的日子。

每一天，我們反覆地過著相同的生活。我們到學校或公司，一而再、再而三地做著必須要做的事情。很多時候，我們遺忘了自己真正想做什麼，又是在什麼時候

感到快樂。當這樣的現實生活一再重複，我們也在不知不覺中，連人生燦爛耀眼的瞬間是在什麼時候，都不復記憶。

每碰到這種時候，我就會想像自己置身於蓊鬱的森林。我會抹去那些勉強自己反覆做討厭事情的生活痕跡，搖身變成畫中的少女，與森林中的動物們快樂地玩耍跑跳，或者提著美味可口的茶點去野餐，最後仰望著漆黑夜空的繁星，向一天道別。但願，跟我一樣疲於生活的人們，這本《成為你的森林》能成為各位稍作歇息的一座小公園。

每個人的心中，都藏著一名蓊鬱森林中的小少女。宛如取出兒時讀過的童話書、再次展讀一般，願這本書也能帶給你愉快的休憩時光。

——Aeppol

Content

如初雪般珍貴，又如回憶般溫暖

寫給思念的你

現在，就跟隨少女的腳步，
走入這片遙遠的蓊鬱森林，
到森林小屋作客吧。

居住於森林中的少女

숲속에 사는 소녀.
초록이 우거진 외딴 숲,
소녀를 따라 숲속 집으로 놀러오세요.

The Girl in the Forest
Come and visit the girl who lives
in a house in a remote, green forest.

珍藏
風景

清朗的天氣，

徐徐的微風，

以及，你凝視著我的眼神……。

我將今天珍貴的瞬間

記錄並珍藏於畫布之上。

風경을 담아

맑은 날씨.

잔잔한 바람.

나를 바라보는 너의 눈빛…….

오늘의 소중한 순간을 화폭에 담아 기록해요.

With a Beautiful Scenery

It is one fine breezy day,

and your eyes are looking at me.

I capture this precious moment within my drawing.

陽光的味道

在陽光充足的日子，
我將衣服晾在院子裡，
從鬆軟的衣物之中，散發出陽光的味道，
令人喜愛極了。

햇볕 냄새

햇살 좋은 날, 마당에 빨래를 널어요.
뽀송하게 잘 마른 빨래에 밴 햇볕 냄새가
나는 너무 좋아요.

The Scent of the Sun

On a fine sunny day, I hang laundry in the yard.
I love the scent of the sun on dried laundry.

迷你
夏季庭園

在不知不覺中，水藍色繡球花、各式玫瑰、
紫羅蘭與勿忘草已變得如此迷人。
每逢初夏，就能遇見這一小片清新的小庭園。

작은 여름 정원

어느새 탐스러워진 푸른 수국과 색색의 장미, 제비꽃과 물망초.
초여름이면 만나볼 수 있는 싱그러운 작은 정원.

Tiny Summer Garden

With blue hydrangeas, red roses, violets and forget-me-nots,
early summer greets us at the tiny garden.

森林的聲音

初夏之始。

轉瞬變綠的樹葉沙沙作響，

不知名的山中鳥兒以悅耳的歌聲吟唱，

偶有小動物撥開草葉，忙碌覓食。

我靜靜地傾聽那陣窸窣的聲響，不禁想著，

也許，未經過任何修飾、最原始天然的森林音樂，

便是這種聲音吧？

숲의 소리

여름의 초입.

금세 푸르러진 나무의 잎들이 사부작거리고

이름 모를 산새들이 고운 목소리를 뽐내며 지저귀는 소리.

이따금 작은 동물들이 먹이를 찾느라 나뭇잎을 헤집고

부산스럽게 움직이는 소리를 가만히 듣고 있노라면

꾸미지 않고 자연스러운

숲의 음악이 이런 것일까 싶습니다.

The Sound of the Forest

It's the beginning of summer.

The green leaves are whistling in the wind.

Unknown mountain birds are singing lovely sounds.

To the sound of small animals

looking for food among the leaves,

I come to think that this might be the music of the forest

—natural and unadorned.

我
心中的
彩虹

只要有令人愉快的故事與歡笑聲，

讓自己心煩意亂、鬱鬱寡歡的事情，也能隨即忘得一乾二淨。

就算內心的天空烏雲密布，也很快就會升起一道美麗彩虹。

내 마음속 무지개

싫었던 일도 우울했던 일도

즐거운 이야기와 웃음 하나면 금방 잊어버리곤 해요.

마음속 하늘에 먹구름이 끼었다가도 금방

무지개가 떠오릅니다.

A Rainbow in My Heart

Happy stories and laughter

release me from all that I hate and all that make me gloomy.

They clear the dark clouds in my heart, leaving a rainbow instead.

與你同行

巨木高聳入天，我和你走在筆直的森林小徑上，

一陣又一陣涼風，從樹木之間迎面吹來，

我

真的

好喜歡，

和你一起走在這條路上。

함께 걷는 길

키 큰 나무들 사이로 곧게 뻗은 숲길을 걸어요.

이따금씩 나무 사이로 나부끼는 시원한 바람을 맞으며

너와 함께 걷는 이 길이

온통

사랑스러워요.

Walking Together

We walk among tall trees.

Facing fresh winds coming through the trees,

I just love the way

we walk together.

猶如
向日葵
般

就算夏日的陽光如此熾熱，那也無妨。

偶爾，我就是想默默守候在那個地方，

靜靜地，當個仰望太陽的人，

猶如一朵向日葵般。

해바라기처럼

뜨거운 여름 햇살이라도 상관없어요.

때로는 묵묵히 그 자리를 지키고서

가만히 해를 바라보는 사람이 되고 싶어요.

마치 한 송이 해바라기처럼요.

Like a Sunflower

I don't care about the hot weather and the strong sunlight.

Sometimes, I just want to stand still

and look at the sun.

As if I were a sunflower.

吃西瓜
的
日子

我以雙手捧著香甜欲滴的西瓜大快朵頤，

就連嘴角沾到了也渾然不覺，

不一會兒，

熱氣也跟著輕飄飄地消散了。

수박 먹는 날

먹음직스러운 수박을 두 손 가득 집어 들고
입가에 묻는 것도 모른 채 열심히 먹다 보면
어느새
더위도 훌훌 가버려요.

Watermelon Day

While I hold a huge piece of watermelon with both of my hands
and enjoy it without knowing that it's smeared all around my mouth,
the heat leaves my mind completely.

凝視著
水族箱

繽紛多彩的魚兒輕搖尾巴，游來游去，

水波盪漾，氣泡咕嚕咕嚕浮起，

我靜靜地凝視著水族箱，

感覺自己就像置身在海洋之中。

어항을 들여다보면

작게 헤엄치며 돌아다니는 색색의 물고기들과

일렁이는 물결, 보글보글 피어오르는 공기방울.

어항을 가만히 들여다보면,

마치 바닷속에 있는 것 같은 느낌이 들어요.

Looking into the Fishbowl

Colorful tiny fishes swimming about,

tiny waves, and rising bubbles.

I Look into the fishbowl,

and I feel like I'm in the ocean.

來杯逗號

疲憊的時候，

稍微

休息片刻也不錯。

쉼표 한 잔

힘들면
잠시
쉬어가도 좋아요.

A Cup Filled with Commas

It's okay to take a break when you're tired.

需要
甜蜜滋味
的日子

腦海中不斷地浮現甜點的模樣，

像是以草莓點綴的鮮奶油蛋糕、草莓泡芙、

暢快沁涼的草莓冰沙……。

今天，是個需要甜蜜滋味的日子。

달콤함이 필요한 날

딸기가 얹어진 생크림 케이크,

딸기 슈크림 빵, 시원한 딸기 스무디…….

디저트가 끝없이 생각나는,

오늘은 달콤함이 필요한 날입니다.

In Need of Sweets

A piece of cake with strawberries on top,

a strawberry cream puff, an ice-cold strawberry smoothie . . .

With thoughts and thoughts of dishes of dessert,

today is a day in need of sweets.

飛高、還要更高

將風箏放飛在那蔚藍的高空，

飛高、

還要更高，

直到它能碰上雲朵。

높이 더 높이

푸른 하늘 저 멀리 연을 띄워 날려요.

구름에 닿을 만큼

높이

더 높이요.

Higher and Higher

Let's fly a kite.

Let's fly it higher and higher so that it can touch the clouds.

坐在窗邊

當我不經意地靠坐在窗戶旁，

雙腿的長度足以碰到地面；

當我的雙腳尺寸，

足以吻合有些過大的室內拖鞋；

當我不需要墊起腳尖，

就能取下高架上的物品時，

是不是就意味著，

我成了我希望變成的大人呢？

창가에 앉아

무심코 창가에 걸터앉았을 때 다리가 땅에 닿을 만큼 길었으면.

조금은 큰 실내용 슬리퍼가 딱 맞을 만큼 발이 커진다면.

높은 선반의 물건을 꺼낼 때

까치발을 들지 않아도 될 만큼 충분히 키가 크다면.

그만큼 자라나면 나는 내가 바라는 어른이 되어 있을까요?

Seated on the Windowsill

If my legs were long enough to reach the ground when I sit on the windowsill,

if my feet were big enough to fit the slightly big indoor slippers,

if I were tall enough to reach the shelf without a tiptoe,

would I be a grown-up just as I wished for?

未知的
門

在森林中溜達時，我遇上了一棵巨樹。

它，會不會是

通往另一個世界的通道呢？

미지의 문

숲에서 거닐던 중 커다란 나무를 만났어요.

이곳은 혹시

다른 세계로 가는

통로가 아닐까요?

Mysterious Door

I stumbled upon a large tree.

Could it be a passage to an unknown world?

如果
我變成了
長髮姑娘

如果我受困於高塔之中，

你會不會攀爬長長的辮子，上來看我呢？

만약 라푼젤이 된다면

만약 내가 높은 탑 속에 갇혀 있다면

너는 나를 위해 머리 타래를 타고 올라와줄까?

Imagination #1

If I Were to Become Rapunzel

If I were locked up inside a tall tower,

I wonder if you'd come for me and climb up my braids.

與
小王子一起

今晚，我們將越過燈火閃爍的城市，

以及湛藍的夜空，

飛往你居住的行星。

어린왕자와 함께

오늘 밤 우리는 불빛이 반짝이는 도시,

푸른 밤하늘을 지나

네가 사는 행성으로 날아갈 거야.

Imagination #2

With the Little Prince

Tonight, we will pass the city of bright lights,

cross the dark blue night sky, and fly away to your planet.

夜間飛行

在無法入眠的夜晚，

彼得潘飛進了我的房間，

而我，欣然地牽起了他的手。

我們縱身越過了有煙囪的屋頂、一座座高山，

也飛過無數的星辰，

我們輕盈地翱翔，

最後來到藍月的面前。

밤의 비행

잠이 오지 않던 밤,

방으로 날아든 피터팬의 손을

나는 선뜻 잡았습니다.

굴뚝이 있는 지붕과 높은 산을 훌쩍 넘고,

수많은 별들을 지나

푸른 달의 코앞까지

우리는 가볍게 날아올랐습니다.

Imagination #3

Flight of Night

On a sleepless night, Peter Pan flies into my room

and I gladly hold the hand he lends.

Over chimneyed rooftops and high mountain tops,

across countless stars and facing the blue moon upfront,

we flew adrift with ease.

少女與
魔豆

第二天起床一看，

發現種在前院的樹木已長到雲端上。

如果我沿著樹木攀爬，

上頭會有什麼樣的世界等著我呢？

소녀와 콩나무

다음 날 일어나 보니

집 앞 공터에 심은 나무가

하늘 높이 자라 있었어요.

나무를 타고 올라가면

어떤 세상이

나를 반길까요?

Imagination #4

A Girl and a Beanstalk

The next morning, the beanstalk in the yard had grown up to the sky.

What kind of world would welcome me if I climbed up to the sky?

可疑的
蘋果

這顆蘋果，

真的能吃下去嗎？

어떤 상상 #5

수상한 사과

이 사과,

먹어도 되는 걸까요?

Imagination #5

A Suspicious Apple

Is this apple truly safe to eat?

有一天，我變小了

你是否曾經

被困在一個無路可走的地方呢？

束手無策的我，

感到自己比平時更加渺小了。

不過，我依然會耐心等待

一個

替我指引出路的人。

어느 날 작아진 내가

사방에 길이 없는 곳에

갇혀본 적이 있나요?

아무것도 할 수 없는 나는

평소보다 아주 작은 존재처럼 느껴지지요.

그래도 기다려볼 거예요.

길이 있는 곳으로 나를 이끌어줄

그 누군가를.

Imagination #6

When I Feel Small

Have you ever been trapped in a place that has no way out?

I feel very small, incapable of anything. But still, I will wait.

I will wait for someone who will lead me to a way out.

來去度假吧

就算無法立刻跑到涼爽的海洋也沒關係，

那就翻開描繪秀麗景致的書頁，

想像自己徜徉其中吧！

那麼，蔚藍大海就會

在你眼前浮現，

栩栩如生地。

휴가를 떠나요

시원한 바다로 당장 떠나지 못해도 좋아요.

멋진 풍경이 그려진 책의 페이지를 펼치고,

그곳에 있다고 상상해보는 거예요.

푸른 바다가 눈앞에 있는 것처럼

생생하게

떠오를 거예요.

Let's Go on a Vacation

It's alright if we don't make our way to the cool ocean right now.

Open a book with a scenic illustration,

and imagine you are there.

In vivid details,

you will see yourself in front of the blue sea.

某個
下雨天

下了一整天的雨，

伴隨著由雨滴串起的樂聲，

我們

靜靜地

望著

窗外。

어느 비 내리던 날

하루 종일 비가 계속 내리던 날.

빗방울이 들려주는 음악소리에

가만히

창밖만

바라보았던

우리.

One Rainy Day

On a rainy day,

we stayed next to the window

and enjoyed the song from the raindrops.

喜歡
雨後放晴的
天空

一連下了好幾天的雨，

直到今天早晨，雨勢才逐漸消停。

森林處處還垂掛著雨滴，

每一片小小的葉片，

都顯得更加翠綠與明亮了。

我看著投射在小池塘的清朗天空，

開心地露出了笑容。

비 갠 하늘이 좋아

한동안 계속되던 비가

오늘 아침에서야 겨우 잠잠해졌어요.

빗방울 머금은 숲은

작은 이파리 하나하나

더욱 푸르고 빛이 나네요.

숲속 작은 샘에 비친 맑게 갠 하늘을 보니

반짝 웃음이 납니다.

I Love the Sky After the Rain

The rain had lasted for days, and finally stopped this morning.

The forest holds the fallen rain, and each leaf is ever filled with life and light.

I look at the sky, reflected in a small pond, and I smile with its shimmer.

紙飛機

雖然這是一只用紙摺成的飛機，

但我多麼希望，

它能夠乘著風，越過綠意盎然的山頭與田野，

自由自在地翱翔，

飛到

我看不見的天際為止。

종이비행기

비록 종이로 접어 만든 비행기지만

불어오는 바람을 타고 푸른 산과 들판을 지나

내 눈이 닿지 않는 하늘 끝까지

자유롭게

날아갔으면 좋겠어요.

Paper Plane

Although it is made of paper,

I hope it rides the wind,

over the mountains and fields,

and reaches the sky above, beyond my sight.

捨不得
分 開

漫天鋪蓋的晚霞之所以格外緋紅，

或許是因為太陽捨不得分開，

所以才鬧了一頓脾氣。

헤어지기 아쉬워

노을 지는 하늘이 유독 붉은 것이

헤어짐을 아쉬워하는

해님의 투정 어린 인사 같아요.

Unwilling to Part

The sky is fiery when the sun sets down

as if the sun is fussing a farewell

for its unwilling parting.

害怕一個人
的夜晚

令人心慌慌的夜晚，

就好像鬼魂會突然從哪兒冒出來似的。

即便如此，我好慶幸

有你在我身旁。

혼자 있기 무서운 밤

어디선가 불쑥

귀신이 나올 것만 같아 무서운 밤.

그래도 내 곁에 네가 있어서

다행이야.

A Night Too Scary to Stay Alone

I'm scared of ghosts tonight.

But your presence relieves me of any fright.

獨一無二的星星

在數不清的星辰之中，

唯有一顆星星，映入了我的眼簾。

你知道嗎？

於我而言，你便是這樣的存在。

단 하나의 별

수많은 별들 중
내 눈에 들어오는 단 하나의 별.
알고 있니?

너는 내게 그런 존재야.

The Only Star

The one star that catches my eye
out of countless others.
You know what?
That's what you are to me.

你是安慰，
是禮物，
是愛

就像是完成作品的最後一片拼圖，

你是安慰，是禮物，是愛，

填補了我的空缺。

너는 위로, 너는 선물, 너는 사랑

완성되지 않은 퍼즐의 마지막 조각처럼

나의 빈틈을 채워주는

너는 위로, 너는 선물, 너는 사랑.

You Are Words of Comfort, You Are a Gift, You Are Love.

Like the last piece of an incomplete puzzle,

you fill in the missing part of me.

You are words of comfort, you are a gift, you are love.

感受秋日

若是閉上雙眼，蔚藍的天空就會更加鮮明呢。

秋日，靜悄悄地飄落在我頭上。

가을 느끼기

눈을 감으면 더욱 선명한 푸른 하늘.

가을이 내 위로 가만히 내려앉아요.

Feeling Autumn

The blue sky becomes even clearer when I close my eyes.

Autumn falls and sits upon me.

神奇的
沙發

你曾聽說過神奇的沙發嗎？

當秋風溫柔吹拂，

只要倚靠著它，便會甜甜地進入夢鄉。

今天，我又再一次地，

抗拒不了沙發的魔力，

沉沉地睡著了。

신기한 소파

가을바람이 솔솔 불어올 때

기대어 앉기만 하면 스르륵 잠이 드는

신기한 소파 이야기를 들어보셨나요.

오늘도 그 소파 때문에 할 수 없이

잠이 들고 말았네요.

Marvelous Sofa

Have you heard of a marvelous sofa

that brings you to sleep

when you sit on it on a breezy autumn day?

Today, again, I gave in to its enchantment

and spent my day in slumber.

尋找相似
的雲朵

秋高氣爽，飄浮的白雲片片。

我發現自己在不知不覺間，

尋找起

與你相似的雲朵。

닮은 구름 찾기

높고 푸른 가을 하늘, 두둥실 흘러가는 흰 구름 떼.

어느새 당신과 닮은 구름을 찾고 있는

나를

발견하곤 해요.

A Look-alike Cloud

Under a flock of white clouds floats about in the blue, autumn sky,

I find myself hoping to discover

a cloud that looks just like you.

來一口
紅透的
秋天

我小心翼翼地摘下兩顆紅透的蘋果。

那清新的果香令人垂涎欲滴，

於是，我也不自覺地咬下了

一口秋天。

붉게 익은 가을 한 입

빨갛게 잘 익은 사과를 하나둘 조심스레 땁니다.

향긋한 내음에 군침이 돌아

나도 모르게 가을을 한 입

베어 먹었어요.

A Bite of Ripened Red Autumn

I carefully pick a couple of red, ripe apples.

Unable to resist the mouth-watering fragrance,

I took a bite out of autumn.

以
雙手
裝盛秋天

我在秋日的街道上，

遇見了火紅的楓葉、銀杏葉、橡子與松果⋯⋯。

我以雙手盛起滿滿的秋意，將它們收藏在心中。

聽說，如果能夠接到落葉，願望就能實現呢！

於是，我們很認真地想抓取落葉，

完全沒留意到時間過了多久。

或許，季節隨即會轉身離開，

但此刻的心情，將會為我留下愉快美好的回憶。

두 손에 가을 담기
가을 길에서 만난 붉은 단풍과 은행잎, 도토리, 솔방울 들⋯⋯.
두 손 가득 가을을 담아 마음속에 간직합니다.
떨어지는 낙엽을 손으로 받으면 소원이 이뤄진다는 말에
우리는 시간 가는 줄 모르고 낙엽 잡기에 열심이었어요.
계절은 금세 지나가도 지금 이 기분은
나에게 즐거운 추억으로 남을 거예요.

Holding Autumn with My Two Hands

Red maple leaves, ginkgo leaves, acorns,

and cones I met on the autumn street . . .

I hold autumn with my two hands and cherish it in my heart.

"Catch a falling leaf and your wish becomes true", we heard,

so we tried to catch them without being aware of time passing.

The season may swiftly pass, but this feeling will remain as a happy memory.

秋雨

天氣變得涼颼颼的，

此時，降下了一場令人欣喜的甘霖。

楓葉越發緋紅，銀杏葉也變得更加澄黃，

就連我的心，也沾染了秋天的色澤。

가을 비

제법 쌀쌀해진 날씨에

반가운 단비가 찾아왔어요.

단풍은 더 붉고 은행잎은 더 노랗게

내 마음도 함께

젖어들어가네요.

Autumn Rain

When the weather started to get chilly,

a welcomed rain arrived.

With its touch, foliage turns red and ginkgo deepens in yellow.

In turn, my heart soaks in autumn as well.

風之歌

靜靜地，側耳傾聽
那無數樹葉飄舞的聲音，
會不會是，風兒想借著它們的身體，
向我們訴說故事呢？

바람의 노래
가만히 귀 기울여 들어보세요.
나뭇가지의 수많은 잎들이 한들거리는 소리는,
바람이 그들의 몸을 빌려
전하고픈 이야기가 아닐까요?

Song of the Wind
Be still and open your ears.
Could it be that the wind is telling us a story
by rattling the leaves on countless branches?

製作餅乾

麵粉、雞蛋、砂糖、杏仁與巧克力脆片……。

製作餅乾時的快樂，

令我情不自禁地吹起了口哨。

只要將烤好的餅乾裝入美麗的罐子內包裝好，

它就會成為世界上獨一無二的美味禮物。

但願，一小片餅乾

也能讓你的心變得甜滋滋的。

쿠키를 만들어요

밀가루와 달걀, 설탕과 아몬드 그리고 초코칩…….

쿠키를 만드느라 즐거워서 나도 모르게 휘파람이 나와요.

잘 구워진 쿠키를 예쁜 통에 담아 포장하면,

세상에 하나뿐인 맛있는 선물이 될 거예요.

쿠키 한 조각에 당신의 마음도

달달해졌으면 해요.

Let's Bake Some Cookies

Flour, eggs, sugar, almonds, and chocolate chip . . .

The joy of baking cookies blows whistles out of my mouth.

The tasty cookies that are placed in a pretty tin

will be the only delicious gift in the world.

With a bite, I hope your dreams become sweet as well.

在家
待上一天

不必做什麼特別的事情，

只要悠閒地待在家中放鬆，

如此，

不也是愜意自在

又幸福洋溢的一天嗎？

집에서 보낸 하루

별다른 일을 하지 않아도 좋아요.

그저 집 안에서 느긋하게 시간을 보낸다면,

그 또한

편안하고

행복한 하루가 아닐까요?

A Day Spent at Home

You don't need to do anything special.

Isn't simply relaxing at home

another way to spend a comfortable and happy day?

秋日野餐

落葉一片、兩片飄下，

嫣紅奼紫在山腳下蜿蜒，

帶上精心準備的茶點，

一塊好好享受秋日的野餐吧！

가을 소풍

하나둘 떨어지는 낙엽들.

울긋불긋 물든 산자락의 굽이굽이.

정성스레 준비한 다과와 함께

가을날의 소풍을 즐겨봅니다.

An Autumn Picnic

Leaves fall down one after another.

Paths crawl on a brightly colored mountain.

Enjoy this autumn picnic

with snacks prepared with love.

晚霞餘暉

「今天過得怎麼樣呢？」晚霞帶著一臉笑意問我。

但我卻不好意思回答：「我過了很充實的一天！」

因此只好沉默以對。

而後，夕陽悄悄地

　　　　隱沒在山的那一頭，

我靜靜地坐在窗邊，看著晚霞落下，

心，也沒來由地跟著西沉了。

노을 지는 저녁

"오늘 하루 어땠나요?" 밝은 눈으로 물어보는 노을에게

'오늘은 참 보람찬 하루였어요!'

'충실한 하루를 보냈어요!'

라고 답하기 부끄러워 침묵으로 응대하자

슬그머니 고개 너머로

사라지고 맙니다.

가만히 창가에 앉아 지는 노을을 바라보고 있노라면

괜스레 마음 한편이 시큰해집니다.

Sun-setting Evening

"How was your day?" cheerfully asked the setting sun. But I was too embarrassed
to say "I had a fulfilling and productive day" and instead replied by silence.
Then the sun, also silently, slid away over the hill. As I sat still by the window,
watching him go away, my heart sank a little in my chest.

深夜漫步

越過大波斯菊盛開的山丘與羊腸小徑，

我，走入了一片白樺樹林，

靠著一盞燈火照亮漆黑的山路，持續前行。

有你成為我心中的一道光芒，

不管面對任何黑暗，我都不害怕。

한밤의 산책

코스모스가 핀 언덕 너머 꼬불꼬불한 오솔길을 지나

흰 자작나무 숲에 닿아요.

캄캄한 산길을 램프 하나에 의지한 채

걷고 또 걸어요.

당신이 내 마음의 빛이 되어주었기에

어떤 어둠도 두렵지 않아요.

A Midnight Stroll

Over the cosmos-covered hills and along the long, winding trails,

I walk into a white birch forest.

Only with a lamp to lead the way,

I walk and walk down the dark forest.

I'm no longer afraid of darkness

for you are the light of my heart.

觀賞星星

漫天的星斗，好似一席閃閃發亮的地毯，

讓人出神凝望，毫無察覺時光的流逝。

現在的你，

是否

也看著相同的天空呢？

별을 구경해요

하늘 가득 빛나는 별들은 마치 반짝이는 융단 같아서

시간 가는 줄 모르고 하염없이 바라보아요.

당신도

지금

나와 같은 하늘을 보고 있을까요?

Watching Stars

Looking at the stars shining in the sky like a carpet of glitter,

not knowing how time passes by,

I sit and wonder if we're looking at the same sky right now.

我
離不開　棉被

雖然，轉眼間天色已亮，

但我的身子還想待在暖和的被窩裡⋯⋯。

無論我再怎麼努力，依舊無法離開棉被。

我才不管吵得要命的鬧鐘，

以及輕叩窗戶的清晨陽光呢。

棉被裡這麼暖和舒適，

我決定要再多睡一會。

이불 속에서 벗어날 수가 없어요

어느새 밝은 아침이 되었는데도

몸은 아직 침대 위 포근한 이불 속에⋯⋯.

아무리 노력해도 이불 속에서 벗어날 수가 없어요.

시끄럽게 울리는 알람 시계도,

창문을 두드리는 아침 햇살도 모른 척할래요.

이불 속이 이리도 포근한 걸요?

나는 좀 더 자야겠어요.

Can't Get Out of Bed

The sun has dawned, but I still can't get out of my warm bed.

No matter how hard I try, I just can't get out.

I'll ignore the ringing alarm clock

and the sunlight knocking on my window.

It's so comfortable here in my bed!

Oh well, I'm going back to sleep.

清掃落葉

時間的痕跡落在了秋日的地面上，
要是放任它們不管，之後恐怕會寸步難行吧？
為了迎接下個季節的來臨，
先將它們掃到一旁吧！

낙엽 쓸기
가을 내내 땅 위로 떨어져 내린 시간의 흔적들.
그대로 두면 앞으로 나아가기 어렵겠지요.
다음 계절을 맞이하기 위해
길 한편으로 쓸어두어요.

Sweeping Fallen Leaves
We sweep aside traces of time
that has piled up all autumn long as we prepare for winter.

想
躲起來
的一天

今天心情好低落喔。

就連明亮的陽光

都令人感到討厭。

숨고 싶은 날

기분이 울적한 하루.

밝은 햇살마저

미운 그런 날.

Escape

What a moody and gloomy day.

Even the bright sunlight seems obnoxious today.

花

每一種花兒，盛開的季節各有不同，

不管是何種花朵，

只要季節來臨，受到了呼喚，

就會接二連三地綻放花蕾。

請別擔心，很快地，

你也會迎來花開的日子。

꽃

꽃은 피어나는 계절이 저마다 다릅니다.

어떤 꽃이든 계절에 따라 제 이름이 불리면

저마다 하나둘 꽃망울을 터뜨리는 법이지요.

걱정 말아요.

당신도 곧

꽃피울 때가 올 거예요.

Flowers

Each flower blooms in different seasons.

Every flower takes its turn

when its name is called in its own season.

Don't worry.

You will bloom soon, too.

山坡上
的樹木

一棵山丘上的合抱之木

曾經炫耀它那茂密的綠葉，

可是，隨著時間的流逝，

如今，它只留下了光禿禿的樹枝。

나무 이야기 #1

언덕 위의 나무

언덕 위 푸른 잎을 자랑하던 아름드리나무 한 그루.
시간이 흘러 어느덧 앙상한 가지만 남게 되었어요.

Tree story #1

A Tree on a Hill

A large tree on a hill showing off its green leaves.
But now, as time passed by, only bare branches linger.

白雲
之樹

微風吹來一朵雲團，

掛在了樹枝上，

使它成了一棵白葉茂密的白雲之樹。

有了新葉之後，

樹木似乎心情很愉快地

正在搖頭晃腦呢。

나무 이야기 #2

구름 나무

바람결에 흘러가는 뭉게구름이 나뭇가지에 걸려.

하얀 잎이 무성한 구름나무가 되었어요.

새 잎사귀들을 갖게 된 나무는

기분 좋은 듯 가지를 흔들어 보입니다.

Tree story #2

A Cloud Tree

Large cotton clouds drifting in the wind were caught by a branch,

and formed a cloud tree full of white leaves.

The tree with newly born leaves, as if it's happy,

waves its branches about.

如果我
變成了
大人

變成大人後的我，

會是何種模樣呢？

어른이 된다면
어른이 된
나는 어떤 모습일까?

When I Become a Grown-up
What would I be like when I become a grown-up?

或許看似
微不足道

有時候，只要我們稍微改變視角，

便能感受到眼睛所看不見的事物。

就像是，我們看著風車旋轉，

便能感受到，風的存在。

아주 작게만 보일지라도

눈에 보이진 않지만 조금만 시선을 달리하면

느껴지는 것들이 있어요.

마치 바람개비가 도는 것을 보고

바람을

느끼는 것처럼요.

All the Small Things

Sometimes we can feel the unseen

if we change our perspective.

Just like we can feel the presence of the wind

when a pinwheel spins.

充滿芳香
之人

花朵的香氣，由風兒來傳遞；

人的香氣，則由心靈來傳遞。

當我們分隔兩地，我便思念起對方，

當對方在我身旁，我感到幸福洋溢；

當我們一起做些什麼時，總有一股芳香暖意縈繞。

因為有這些人在我身旁，

今天也充滿了芬芳。

향기로운 사람

꽃의 향기는 바람이 전하고

사람의 향기는 마음이 전합니다.

멀리 있으면 그립고, 곁에 있으면 행복한 사람.

함께하면 늘 향기로운 따뜻한 사람.

그런 이들이 곁에 있어

오늘도 향기롭습니다.

A Lovely Scent

The wind delivers the fragrance of flowers,

and the heart delivers the fragrance of others.

The person I miss when we're apart,

and the person who makes me happy when we're together.

A warm person who brings along a lovely scent.

People with such scent make my day delightful and pleasant.

一步、兩步，

隨著雪地上的腳印增加，

我們走入了冬日的正中央。

如初雪般珍貴，
又如回憶般溫暖

첫눈처럼 소중한,
추억만큼 따스한
한 발, 두 발
흰 눈밭에 찍힌 발자국만큼
우리는 그렇게 겨울의 한가운데에
들어와 있었습니다.

Precious as the First Snow,
Warm as a Happy Memory
A footprint, two footprints,
following each footprint into the white snowfield,
we've arrived at the deep center of winter.

初雪

為了祝賀冬日的來臨，

雪白的花粉簌簌紛飛，

不一會兒，轉成了鵝毛大雪，

整座山頭，覆上了白茫茫的一片。

腳步落在白雪地毯上時，

會嘎吱、嘎吱地，發出令人愉悅的聲響，

於是，我們迎接著落下的白雪，

雀躍地四處跑著、跳著。

첫눈

겨울에 접어든 것을 축하하는

하얀 꽃가루가 부슬부슬 흩날리더니

어느새 함박눈으로 변해

온 산을 하얗게 덮었습니다.

눈 카펫을 밟으면

뽀득뽀득 기분 좋은 소리가 나서

우리는 내리는 눈을 맞으며

즐겁게 뛰어다녔답니다.

First Snow

White pollen scatters around and celebrates winter's arrival.
Soon, they turn to a flock of thick snow and cover the mountain, whole.

We step on the carpet of snow, and to the peasant crunches below our feet,
we run in joy under the falling snow.

編織

在陽光滿溢的房間裡，

我拾起宛如陽光般橙黃的毛線，

一針、一針地勾著。

想到那人收到禮物後，臉上欣喜的表情，

我也不禁漾開了笑容。

滿滿的心意，都裝在了這裡頭，

但願你，能過上一個暖冬。

뜨개질

햇살 가득한 공간에서

한 올 한 올 뜨개질을 해요.

볕을 닮은 노란색 털실을 골라

한 코 한 코 엮다 보면,

받을 이의 환한 웃음이 생각나

절로 미소가 지어져요.

따뜻한 겨울을 보내길 바라는 마음을

가득 담았어요.

Knitting

In a room filled with sunlight,

I pick up a thread—yellow like a little star, and start knitting.

With each needle,

I think of the smile when the gift is delivered and smile along myself.

I also pack my regards wishing a warm winter inside.

夜晚的
小訪客

親愛的小精靈們，

我已經擺放了熱好的牛奶與茶點，

能不能，在你們享用完畢之後，

替我解決桌上尚未編織好的毛線呢？

我留了一封信之後，便進入了夢鄉。

結果，嬌小又善良的精靈們真的在夜晚現身了！

我深怕會打擾他們，所以偷偷地躲起來看了一會，

接著又躡手躡腳地跑回了床上。

작은 밤 손님

Dear 요정님들

따뜻하게 데운 우유와 다과를 두었으니

맛있게 드시고 테이블 위의 뜨개질거리를

해결해주지 않으시겠어요?

편지를 써두고 잠이 들었는데,

작고 친절한 요정님들이 정말로 밤에 나타나주었어요.

방해가 될까 봐 몰래 바라보다가

살금살금 침대로 돌아갑니다.

Lovely Visitors at Night

"Dear fairies,

I left you some warm milk and cookies.

Help yourself and please take care of

the rest of the knitting on the table?"

I left the letter and went to bed,

and the kind fairies really came out!

I didn't want to interrupt, so after peeking for a while,

I snuck back to bed.

就算天氣冷颼颼的，
也要去露營！

冬天到了，天氣真是寒風刺骨呀，

不過，去露營就更有氣氛了呢。

我將地瓜與香腸放在火爐上，

一邊烤著棉花糖來吃，一邊靜候它們熟透。

把肚子填得飽飽的之後，

我們悄聲細語，與彼此分享祕密。

我們只顧著沉浸在歡樂的時光中，

絲毫沒發現，夜都這麼深了呢！

쌀쌀해도 캠핑!

겨울이라 날이 무척 쌀쌀하지만

그래서 캠핑하기 더 좋은 것 같아요.

화로에 고구마와 소시지를 올리고

다 익을 때까지 기다리며 마시멜로를 구워 먹어요.

배가 가득 부르도록 먹고 난 후에 나누는

소곤소곤 비밀 이야기들.

재미있는 시간을 보내느라

밤이 깊어지는 줄도 몰랐네요!

I Can't Give Up on Camping Even If It's Cold!

The winter brings cold weather, but that makes camping even better.

I put sweet potatoes and sausages on the grill, and I bake marshmallows while I wait.

After eating as much as I can, we whisper to each other our secrets.

We have so much fun and joy that we are unaware of how late the night falls.

書

書中的未知世界過於浩瀚無邊，
使得生活在渺小世界中的我，
顯得越發渺小了。
即便如此，
當我閱讀了一本、兩本……
隨著書籍量的增加，
我那些渺小的想法，
似乎也會隨之成長。

책

책 속엔 내가 모르는 세상이 너무도 넓어
이렇게 작은 세계 속의 나는 한참이나 작아 보이지만
한 권, 두 권
읽은 책들이 쌓일수록

나의 작은 생각들도
조금은 성장한 것 같아요.

Books

Books contain parts of the world I never knew.
Although the tiny world I lived in makes me feel even smaller,
each book I read
helps my thoughts grow taller.

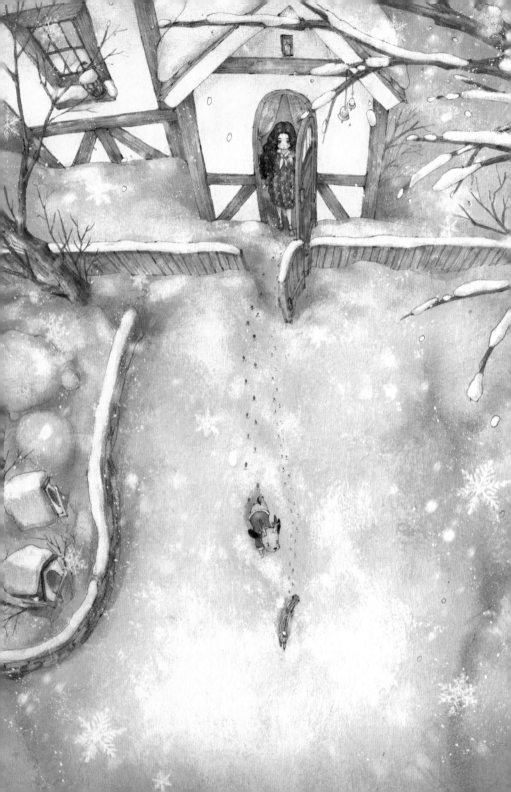

白皚皚
的世界

清晨，

我身穿睡衣，揉著惺忪的雙眼，

打開大門一看，

發現整個世界

變成了一片雪白。

온통 하얀 세상

이른 아침.

잠옷 바람으로 눈 비비며 나와

대문을 열어보니

세상이 온통 하얗게 변해 있어요.

Winter Story #1

A World Covered in White

Early in the morning, I opened the front door,

rubbing my eyes in my pajamas, and found the world covered in white.

雪人家族

我滾動著雪球，

做出了一個雪人。

有大家同心協力，

很快就會有一個雪人大家族了！

눈사람 가족

흰 눈을 뭉치고 굴려

눈사람을 만들어요.

다 함께 힘을 합쳐 만드니

금방 눈사람 대가족이 되었어요.

Winter Story #2

A Family of Snowmen

I rolled the white snow around and made a snowman.

With our efforts combined, we soon made a big family of snowmen.

大半夜
的
拜訪

深夜裡，

我聽見一個微弱的敲門聲，醒了過來。

從小小的門縫裡，雪人探出了頭，

他說：「外面太冷了，我睡不著覺。」

한밤중의 방문

깊은 밤.

작은 노크 소리에 잠이 깼어요.

열린 방문 사이로

빼꼼 고개를 내민 눈사람이 건넨 말.

"밖은 너무 추워서 잠을 잘 수가 없어요."

Winter Story #3

A Late Night Visit

Deep into the night, I woke up to a knock on the door.

Through the doorway, the snowman peeped in and said,

"It's too cold outside and I cannot sleep".

願你，
有個
溫暖的夢

我讓瑟瑟發抖的雪人

鑽進暖烘烘的被窩裡。

我緊緊地擁抱這個無法成眠的孩子，

很快地，他進入了夢鄉。

但願你，能有個溫暖的夢……。

따뜻한 꿈을 꾸기를

추위에 떠는 눈사람을

포근한 이불 속으로 들어오게 했어요.

쉽게 잠을 이루지 못하는 아이를 꼬옥 안아주니

어느새 스르륵 잠이 듭니다.

부디 따뜻한 꿈을 꾸기를……

Winter Story #4

In Hope of Your Warm Sweet Dreams

I offered the shivering snowman a small spot inside my warm, cozy blanket.

I held the sleepless child in my arms and soon the child fell asleep.

I hope you have a warm, sweet dream.

早晨再度來臨

度過一個暖呼呼的夜晚，早晨再度來臨，

陽光從窗戶溜了進來，於是我也跟著醒了。

而睡在我身旁的雪人，早已消失得無影無蹤，

床上，只剩下我為他戴上的帽子與圍巾。

這是

某個冬日清晨發生的事情。

다시 아침

포근한 밤이 지나고 다시 아침.

창을 통해 들어오는 햇살에 잠이 깼어요.

침대 옆자리에 잠들었던 눈사람은 온데간데없이,

내가 걸어준 모자와 목도리만 남아 있었어요.

어느 겨울 아침의

일이었습니다.

Winter Story #5

Morning Comes Again

A cozy night passed and morning came again.

I woke up to the sunlight, coming through the window.

The snowman in my bed had already left—

only the hat and muffler I had provided remained.

This all had happened on one fine day of winter.

溫暖的
針織衫

真的好神奇哦，

只是把脖子包覆住而已，

卻感覺寒冷已離我遠去。

就好像

牽起你的手時，

心底便一陣暖洋洋的。

따뜻한 터틀넥 니트

참 신기한 일이에요.

목을 덮는 것만으로도

추위가 저 멀리 사라지는 느낌이거든요.

당신의 손만 잡아도

마음이 따뜻해지는 것처럼요.

A Warm Knit Turtleneck Sweater

It's so amazing.

Just by covering my neck,

it feels as though the cold retreats away.

Just like holding your hand

warms up my heart.

陰影

只要

在撒落的陽光之間，

有一小片陰影

輕輕地覆在我的眼皮上，

我就能

在那陰影中

安然入睡。

그늘

내리쬐는 햇볕 사이로 작은 그늘이

살포시 내 두 눈을 가려주면

나는 편안히 잠을 잘 수 있어요.

그 그늘 속에서.

The Shade

When a small shade forms between stripes of sunlight,

and softly covers my eyes,

I can fall asleep in ease,

behind the shade.

夜晚，
傳來下雪的
消息

晚上睡不著覺，翻來覆去的時候，

我不經意地往窗外望去，

看見外頭，正無聲地下起雪來。

我快速地在睡衣上披了一件外套，

漫步於白皚皚的雪地上。

一步、兩步，

隨著雪地上的腳印增加，

我們走入了冬日的正中央。

한밤의 눈 소식

잠이 오지 않아 뒤척이던 밤

문득 창밖을 바라보니

소리 없이 눈이 내리고 있었어요.

급하게 잠옷 위에 겨울 외투를 걸쳐 입고

소복이 쌓인 눈길을 걸었습니다.

한 발, 두 발 흰 눈밭에 찍힌 발자국만큼

우리는 그렇게 겨울의 한가운데에 들어와 있었습니다.

Snowy Winter Night

That night, I couldn't sleep and turned in bed.

Then, I looked out the window and it was snowing.

I quickly wore a coat over my pajamas and walked on the fresh snow.

A footprint, two footprints, following each footprint into the white snowfield,

we've arrived at the deep center of winter.

今天的日記

我以優雅的藍色顏料為天空著色，

並描繪我們嬉戲的模樣，

再以細心削好的各色鉛筆

描繪冬日的森林。

我以小巧的字體寫下日記，

但願明天也如同今天一般，

好事滿滿。

오늘의 일기

색이 고운 파란 물감으로 하늘을 담고

그곳에서 뛰놀던 우리 모습도 담아

정성스레 깎아둔

색색의 연필들로 겨울의 숲을 그려요.

작은 글씨로 일기를 씁니다.

내일도 오늘처럼 좋은 일만 가득하기를.

Today's Diary

I'm coloring the sky with fine blue paint

and drawing the winter forest with colorful pencils

that I've sharpened.

After I finish the moment we played with each other,

I add today's diary in small letters.

I hope tomorrow is a delightful day like today.

一起
過聖誕節吧

以各色掛飾點綴的聖誕樹、

彩色繽紛的花環，

以及親手準備的美味餐點，

我在飄雪的窗前、溫馨的壁爐旁，

與好友們開一場愉快的聖誕派對。

如果每天都是聖誕節，那該有多好呢？

如此一來，我們就能每天聚在一塊開派對了！

함께해요, 크리스마스
색색의 오너먼트로 장식한
크리스마스트리와 울긋불긋한 갈런드,
손수 준비한 맛있는 음식들.
눈 내리는 창가, 따뜻한 벽난로 옆에서 친구들과 함께
즐겁게 크리스마스 파티를 해요.

매일이 크리스마스라면 얼마나 좋을까요?
이렇게 다 함께 모여 매일매일 파티를 할 수 있잖아요!

Together on Christmas

Colorful ornaments decorating the Christmas tree, bright garlands,
and home cooked dishes.
Next to a snowy window, in front of a warm fireplace,
I have a fun Christmas party with my friends.

How nice would it be if every day were Christmas?
We can gather every day and party like this!

照進
冬日
樹林間

所謂的朋友，不須任何的言語，

單憑一個眼神，便能得知彼此的心思。

那天午後，照進樹木之間的陽光，

比任何時候都來得溫暖。

겨울나무 사이로

친구란 말하지 않고 눈빛만으로도

서로가 무슨 마음인지 알 수 있는 존재예요.

나무 사이로

비추는 해가

유독 따스한 오후였어요.

Through the Winter Trees

Friends are those who don't need words

and can understand each other with a single glance.

The sun shining through the trees was warmer than ever that afternoon.

別生病了

真希望我能替你生病……。

當你生病時，
我的心就好似碎了一地。

千萬別生病了，好嗎？

아프지 말고
내가 대신 아플 수만 있다면 좋을 텐데…….

당신이 아플 때면
내 마음이 무너져 내리는 것 같아요.

부디 아프지 말아요.

Don't Be Sick

I wish I could be sick in your place.
My heart breaks when you're sick.
Please, please, don't be sick.

馬卡龍
鞦韆

我咬下一口甜甜的馬卡龍，
宛如在天空上盪鞦韆一般，
嘴裡盡是幸福的味道。

마카롱 그네

달콤한 마카롱을 한 입 깨물면,
하늘 높이 그네를 타는 것처럼
행복한 기분이 입안에 가득해요.

A Macaron Swing

When I take a bite of a sweet macaron,
happiness fills my mouth
like I'm riding a swing sky high.

呼喚綠意

好懷念冬天鮮少露臉的綠樹，
於是，我將綠意呼喚到房裡。
被綠色滿滿包圍的房間，
就像是一座
小小的森林。

초록을 불러내요
겨울에 보기 힘든 푸른 나무들이 그리워
방 안에 초록을 불러냈어요.
녹색으로 가득 찬 방이
작은 숲속처럼
느껴집니다.

Calling for Greens

I missed the green trees
that went to hiding during winter.
So I called for greens to come to my room.
My leafy room now feels like a small forest.

星光燦爛

為了今天同樣辛苦一整天的你，

我將夜空中

一閃一閃發亮的星星，

裝盛在裙襬之上。

但願，

當你凝望著令人著迷的閃亮光芒時，

你那疲憊不堪的心，也能再次發光。

별빛 담은
오늘 하루도 수고한 당신을 위해 반짝반짝 빛나는
밤하늘의 저 별들을 치마폭에 담아볼게요.
눈을 뗄 수 없는 반짝임을 바라보며
당신의 지친 마음도 다시
빛을 찾기를.

Filled with Starlight
For you, who worked hard again,
twinkling stars in the sky, I'll try to collect.
After you look into the enchanting light,
I wish your tired heart glows again.

在藍夜
與
凌晨之間

半夜裡，我突然醒了過來。

但我沒有試著再度入睡，

而是披上厚厚的外套，

吐出白白的氣息，爬上了小山丘。

山丘上，黑夜已過，天空迎來了凌晨，

依舊帶著一臉睡意的我，也徹底清醒了。

在藍夜與凌晨之間，

重新誕生的早晨，散發柔和的光芒，

一點一點地，向我靠近。

푸른 밤과 새벽 사이

문득 잠에서 깬 밤.

나는 다시 잠들려 애쓰지 않고

두터운 외투를 걸치고서 작은 언덕에 올랐습니다.

흰 입김을 내며 오른 언덕 위에는

까만 밤이 지나고 새벽을 맞이하는 하늘이

아직 얼굴에 잠이 묻어 있는 나를 완연히 깨웠습니다.

푸른 밤과 새벽 사이.

새로 태어난 아침은 희미한 빛을 내며

조금씩 나에게로 오고 있었습니다.

Between a Blue Night and Dawn

I woke up in the middle of the night. I didn't try to go back to sleep again, but took my overcoat and climbed the hill. On top of the hill, the sky that had sent off the blue night and met with dawn brushed off my lingering drowse.

Between a blue night and dawn, the newly born day softly glows and comes to me slowly.

今年
最後一篇
日記

我掀開了熟悉的日記本，

寫下今年的最後一篇日記，

今年真是充滿了許多令人感謝與幸福的日子呢！

想到即將到來的一年，又會有哪些故事填滿日記本呢？

心臟不禁開始

噗通噗通地跳動。

올해의 마지막 일기

손에 익은 일기장을 펼치고

올해의 마지막 일기를 써 내려가요.

올해에는 정말 고맙고 행복한 일들이 많았지요!

다가올 새해에는 어떤 이야기들로 일기장을 채울까

벌써부터 두근두근해요.

The Last Diary of This Year

I opened my favorite diary

and started to write down the very last diary of this year.

Lots of happy things have happened in this year!

And I'm so excited to start up a new diary with happier stories

in the upcoming year.

許下
新年願望

我將一年的心願寄託在天燈上，
並將它，放飛於高空中。
在漆黑的夜空中，漫天的天燈三三兩兩聚在一塊，
有如星光，照亮了我的心底。
但願每個天燈所懷抱的溫暖願望，
都能在今年實現……。

새해의 소망을 빌어요
한 해의 소원을 풍등에 담아
하늘 위로 올려 보내요.
어두운 밤하늘 위 가득 찬 풍등들이 하나둘 모여
별빛처럼 환하게 나의 마음속에 들어옵니다.
저마다 품고 있는 따뜻한 소망들,
올해엔 꼭 이루어지기를…….

Making My New Year's Wish

I write my new year's wish inside a sky lantern and fly it away.
The night sky gathers the lanterns and lights up my heart
like a sky filled with stars.
Warm wishes kept in each heart.
I hope they all come true this year . . .

長多高了呢？

小時候，每一年

我們都會倚靠牆壁測量身高吧？

雖然現在個子不像當時長得那麼快，

但我仍希望，我們的心

能比去年，多長高一個手掌的距離。

今年，你的夢想長大了多少呢？

在這一年之中，你的心又變得有多寬容呢？

얼마만큼 컸나요?

어릴 때는 벽에 등을 대고 서서 매년 키를 재보았지요.

키는 그때처럼 쑥쑥 크지 않을지라도,

마음은 작년보다 한 뼘 더 자랐으면 좋겠어요.

올해 당신의 꿈은 얼마나 자랐나요?

한 해 동안 당신의 마음은 얼마나 넓어졌나요?

How Much Did You Grow?

We all used to lean against the wall and measure our height.

Although our height doesn't grow as much,

I hope our hearts will grow more than it did last year.

How much did your dreams grow this year?

How much did your heart grow in kindness?

Dear.spring

寫給
思念的你

和煦的陽光、清新的空氣、
淡綠色的幼芽、奼紫嫣紅的花朵、
翩翩起舞的蝴蝶、森林的綠樹⋯⋯
我寫了一封信，獻給思念的春天，
但願你能快快到來。

그리운 너에게
따스한 햇볕과 신선한 공기,
연둣빛 싹과 색색의 꽃들, 나비, 푸른 숲의 나무들.
그리운 봄에게 편지를 씁니다.
어서 네가 오기를.

A Letter to You
Warm sunlight and fresh air,
greenish shoots and colorful flowers, butterflies,
and the trees in a deep forest.
I write a letter to spring.
I hope to see you very soon.

青鳥
捎來的消息

正當冬眠的森林甦醒，
整座山頭披上色彩之際，
從那遠處，飛來一隻青鳥。
牠的嘴上銜著春日的消息，朝我而來，
告訴我
春天已近。

파랑새가 물고 온 소식
겨우내 잠들어 있는 숲이 깨어나
온 산에 색이 입혀질 무렵.
저 멀리서 날아오른 푸른 새 한 마리가
입가에 작은 봄소식을 물고 나에게로 옵니다.
이제 이만큼이나
봄이 가까이에 왔다고.

News From a Blue Bird

By the time the forest wakes up from its slumber
and colors itself with green,
a blue bird comes flying towards me.
It carries the news of spring in his beak—
to show how close spring has come.

微風

一陣暖洋洋的微風吹來，
我的心
乘著蒲公英的孢子，
輕飄飄地飛了起來。

산들바람
포근한 바람결,
민들레 홀씨를 타고

내 마음도 두둥실
날아오릅니다.

The Breeze

A cozy wind blows.
My heart rides on dandelion spores
and floats about.

春花時鐘

花朵，是春之時鐘，

接二連三綻放的花朵，宣告了春天的來臨。

此時此刻，開出了幾點鐘的花朵呢？

봄꽃 시계

하나둘 피어나는 꽃들이 봄을 알려요.

꽃은 봄의 시계.

지금은 몇 시의

꽃이 피어나고 있을까요?

A Clock of Spring Flowers

Blooming flowers are telling us that spring is coming.

Flowers are the clock of spring.

I wonder flowers of what time are blooming now?

玻璃瓶內
的春天

和煦的春天這麼快就來臨了，

對此，薄暮的風或許是眼紅了，

風勢吹得格外地猛烈。

在風兒離去之處，一枝花兒

從充滿春日氣息的花樹上跌落，

我於心不忍，

便以雙手小心翼翼地捧抱著，領它回家。

儘管，它只是一根斷裂的花枝，但插在小小的玻璃瓶內，

頓時，家中充滿了春日的芳香。

유리병 속의 봄

따스한 봄이 벌써 와서 시샘이 났는지

저문 오후 바람은 유독 거세게 불었습니다.

바람이 지나간 자리, 봄기운이 탐스럽게 어린 꽃나무에

가지 하나가 꺾여 있는 것을 그냥 두기 안쓰러워

두 손으로 보듬어 집 안으로 데려왔습니다.

비록 꺾인 꽃나무 가지지만, 작은 유리병에 꽂아두니

집 안 가득 싱그러운 봄기운이 채워집니다.

Spring Inside a Glass Bottle

As if it's jealous that spring is already here, the evening wind was especially harsh. Where the wind had passed by, on a young tree where spring abounds, I couldn't ignore a broken branch of flowers and brought it home gently in my hands. Although it was a broken branch of flowers, I put it in a small glass bottle with water. The house is now filled with fresh spring air.

去野餐
前一天

我將鮮甜的蔬果、整齊切好的三明治、
烤成金黃色的餅乾與麵包，
漂亮地擺放在
我最寶貝的便當盒內。
野餐的前一天，
就和去野餐的日子一樣
令人雀躍萬分！

소풍 가기 전날
신선한 과일과 채소, 세모 반듯한 샌드위치,
노릇노릇 구워진 쿠키와 빵을
아끼는 도시락 통에 예쁘게 담아요.
소풍을 떠나는 날만큼이나
소풍 전날도 즐거워요.

The Day Before a Picnic

Fresh fruits, vegetables, a sandwich in a tidy triangle,
and cookies and bread baked in golden crisp—
I neatly place them in my favorite lunch box.
The day before a picnic is
just as exciting as the picnic itself.

風和日麗的午後

我躺在春意盎然的地毯上，
度過了一個慵懶的午後。
陽光在我的眼皮上輕舞，
剛才讀過的書中段落
還在我腦海中徘徊打轉。
真是一個風和日麗的午後呢！
不須我多做什麼，此時已足夠完美。

포근한 오후

봄빛 담요 위에 누워 나른한 오후를 보내요.
감은 눈 위로 아른거리는 햇살과
방금 읽은 책의 구절이 머릿속을 맴도는
포근한 오후를요.
아무것도 하지 않아도 완벽한 순간이에요.

A Cozy Afternoon

I lay on a blanket of spring and spend a cozy afternoon.
Over my closed eyes, the sunlight dances.
In my mind, passages of the book I just put down pounces.
What a cozy afternoon.
Without me doing anything special, I lay in this perfect moment.

你看我，
我看你

光是看著你的臉，

我的心情就好了起來！

마주 보기

바라만 봐도

기분 좋아지는

너의 얼굴.

Facing Each Other

Your face that delights me by mere sight.

乘著
棉花糖

今天，我想乘著

與棉花糖相似的鬆軟雲朵，

任由風兒

將我忽地吹向某處。

솜사탕을 타고
솜사탕을 닮은 폭신한 구름을 타고
바람이 안내해주는 대로
어디론가 훌쩍
떠나고 싶은 날.

Riding on Cotton Candy
I want to ride on a cloud as fluffy as cotton candy
and depart to wherever the wind takes me
on a day like today.

秋天的湖水

沒有半點漣漪的沉靜湖水，
好似一張清澈的明鏡，
如實地映照出上頭的天空。

有好一會兒，
我靜靜凝望著湖水中飄過的雲朵，
絲毫不覺時間流逝。

거울 호수
잔물결 하나 없이 고요한 호수는 거울처럼 깨끗해서
머리 위의 하늘이 그대로 비쳐요.

그렇게 한참이나
시간 지나는 줄 모르고
호수 속 구름이 지나는 것을 들여다보고 있었습니다.

A Mirror Lake

The lake, still and free of ripples, is as clear as a mirror—
it has a lucid reflection of the sky above.

For quite a while, unaware of time passing by,
I stood and watched the clouds pass by inside the lake.

珍藏記憶

真希望

我能將愉快而珍貴的記憶

珍藏在玻璃瓶裡。

기억을 담아

즐겁고 소중한 기억을

유리병에 담아

보관할 수만 있다면.

Keeping Memories

If only I could keep joyful and precious memories

inside a glass bottle.

我專屬的庭園

不如，就在家中的一小塊空間

打造專屬於我的庭園吧？

綠意盎然的虎尾蘭與清香撲鼻的迷迭香、

舒展身子的常春藤與仙人掌花盆，

再擺上一張小圓桌與座椅，

轉眼間，一間居家咖啡廳於焉完成。

在清新植物的包圍之下，慵懶地啜飲一杯茶，

我那感到些許倦怠乏力的心，

也在不知不覺中，感到祥和與溫暖。

나만의 정원

집 안 작은 공간에

나만의 정원을 만들어보는 건 어떨까요?

푸른 산세베리아와 향기로운 로즈메리.

길게 잎을 늘어트린 아이비와 선인장 화분들.

자그마한 탁자와 의자를 놓아두면

금세 멋진 홈 카페가 만들어져요.

싱그러운 식물들 속에서 느긋하게 차 한 잔을 마시면

조금은 지쳐 있던 내 마음도

어느새 편안하고 따뜻해져요.

A Garden of Your Own

How about making a garden of your own in a small part of your home?
Blue sansevierias and fragrant rosemaries, ivies stemming long and cacti
placed in pots. If you add a small table and some chairs, you can easily
complete a nice home cafe. And if you drink a cup of tea surrounded by
fresh plants, you'll soon be relieved of your small burdens, and feel calm
and relaxed.

春日畫框

淺綠色的新葉、春天的紅花與黃花

隨風飄揚，

小小的蝴蝶與山中鳥兒

朝氣蓬勃地飛來飛去。

當我打開窗戶，望向這片風景，

就好像牆上掛了一幅

由春日描繪的巨大畫框。

봄 그림 액자

연둣빛 새잎과 노랗고 붉은 봄꽃이

바람에 산들거리고

작은 나비와 산새들이 활기차게 오가는 풍경.

창문을 열고 풍경을 바라보고 있으면

마치 봄을 그린 커다란 그림 액자가

걸려 있는 것만 같아요.

A Painting of Spring

A scene of young, green leaves

and spring flowers of yellow and red rustling in the wind,

and small butterflies and mountain birds restlessly flying about.

When I open the window and look at this scene,

it's as if a large painting of spring

were hanging on my wall.

滾來滾去

我趴在柔軟舒適的床上，
隨意翻閱想看的書本，
或者和你閒聊，度過午後時光。
如果突然感到睏了，就打個盹，
醒來之後，再盡情地在床上打滾。

看來呀，要等到晚餐時間，
我才有辦法離開床鋪了。

뒹굴 뒹굴
푹신한 침대 위에 배를 깔고 엎드려
보고 싶은 책을 뒤적거리거나
당신과 사소한 잡담을 하며 오후를 보내요.
문득 졸리면 한숨 자고,
자고 일어나면 또 뒹굴거리고.

아마도 저녁 먹을 시간이 되어서야
침대를 벗어날 수 있을 것 같아요.

Lolling Around

On my soft bed, I lie on my stomach. I spend the afternoon skimming through a book of my interest and sharing some small chats with you. When I feel sleepy I take a short nap, and when I wake up I carelessly loll around. Only when it's time to have dinner is when I think I can escape from my bed.

去旅行

頭戴遮陽帽，穿上方便活動的服裝，

我將小巧的相機、地圖與雨傘放入輕盈的背包內。

雖然聽說一整天都會是大太陽，

但誰曉得呢？總是得未雨綢繆嘛。

想像著，我倆一塊查看地圖的模樣，

現在就雀躍不已了呢！

不管到哪，只要和你在一起，

都一定會是愉快盡興的旅行！

여행을 떠나요

햇볕을 가릴 모자와 활동하기 편한 옷차림,

작은 카메라와 지도, 비를 막아줄 우산 등을

가벼운 배낭에 챙깁니다.

하루 종일 화창하다고는 하지만 혹시 모르는 거니까요.

눈에 익지 않은 지도를 살피며

당신과 여행할 시간이 벌써부터 신나고 기대됩니다.

어디든 당신과 함께라면

분명 즐거운 여행이 될 거예요!

Let's Leave for a Trip

A sun hat, a comfortable wear for activities, a small camera, a map, and an umbrella for unexpected rain are all packed in my light travel bag. Although I heard it would be sunny all day, you never know how it's going to be.

I think of us reading an unfamiliar map, and I'm already excited about traveling with you. If it's with you, wherever it may be, the trip will be filled with joy and excitement!

蓋上
睏意的棉被

春日的午後，

是一道道猩紅色光束

在我的眼皮上輕舞閃動的時刻。

睏意猶如輕盈柔軟的羽毛

飄落，

覆在我的雙眼之上。

졸음 이불

봄의 오후.

눈꺼풀 위로 주홍빛 햇볕이 아른거리는 시간.

새털처럼 가볍고 포근한 졸음이 내 눈을 덮어요.

Blanket of Drowsiness

An afternoon in spring.

The hour of scarlet sunbeams gleaming over my eyelids.

Drowsiness—light and soft as a feather—comes down and covers my eyes.

多花紫藤

我在幽靜的小徑上
遇見了爭妍齊放的多花紫藤，
我沉醉於那花朵的色澤，那香氣，
不自覺地在它的下方
停駐了許久。

등나무 꽃
오솔길에서 만난
보랏빛 흐드러지게 핀 등나무 꽃.
꽃의 색에 취해, 향기에 취해
나도 모르게 한참을
그 아래에 서 있었습니다.

Wisteria Flowers

Wisterias of fully bloomed purple hues greet at a trail.
Immersed in their color, immersed in their scent,
I lost myself standing under them for a long while.

線

有時，我會一再地渴求
某件無法攫取的事物，
明知強求不來，仍不願放掉那條線。

即便曉得，唯有放手了，
我的心才會好過一些。

끈

때론 잡지 못할 그 무언가를 바라고 또 바라
안 되는 걸 알면서도 그 끈을 놓지 못합니다.

손을 놔버리는 것이
마음 편해질 길인 걸 알면서도요.

The String

At times, I yearn for something out of my reach.
I refuse to let go of the string that leads to it,
although I'm aware of the comfort of letting go.

夜空的
雪花球

將你我一同仰望的那片夜空

小心珍藏在內心的雪球裡，

等過上一段時日，再取出來欣賞。

那瞬間如此耀眼，

猶如漫天撒落的美麗星星。

밤하늘 스노볼

너와 나 함께 바라보는 저 밤하늘을

마음속 스노볼에 간직해두었다가

시간이 지나면 그때 다시 꺼내어 봐요.

흩뿌린 듯 아름다웠던 별들의 반짝임,

그 순간을.

A Snow Globe of the Night Sky

The night sky we gazed upon together,

I cherish inside a snow globe in my heart.

I bring it out from time to time and see

that moment of the twinkling stars, scattering about.

落在
院子裡的
　　　流星

某一夜，

有顆小小的流星掉落在前院裡，

原來，那是

從月亮寄來的邀請函。

마당에 떨어진 별똥별

어느 날 밤,

집 앞 마당에 떨어진 작은 별똥별은

달에서 보낸 초대장이었어요.

Invitation from the Moon #1

A Shooting Star in the Yard

The shooting star that fell one night in the yard

was an invitation from the Moon.

到
月亮上
旅行

我將流星掛在小浴缸上頭，

四周的星群便朝這兒靠攏。

浴缸猶如一艘小帆船，

隨著群星的引領，飛向天際。

달로 떠나는 여행

작은 욕조에 별똥별을 매달자

주변으로 친구 별들이 모여들었어요.

욕조는 마치 작은 배처럼

별들이 이끄는 대로 하늘을 날아갔습니다.

Invitation from the Moon #2

A Journey to the Moon

After I hung a shooting star above my small bath tub,

its fellow stars gathered around its presence.

The tub, as if it were a small boat, followed the stars and flew up into the sky.

銀河橋

往上飛了好一會兒，

我們抵達了銀河橋。

我步出浴缸，

一步

一步地

走向月亮。

은하수 다리

한참을 날아올라

우리는 은하수 다리에 도착했어요.

욕조에서 내려와

한 발짝

한 발짝

달을 향해 걸어갑니다.

Invitation from the Moon #3

The Milky Way Bridge

We flew up and up for a while and arrived at the Milky Way bridge.

After climbing out of the tub, we approach the Moon, step by step.

歡迎來到月亮

越過銀河橋之後，

我們終於抵達了月亮。

一隻身披長袍、頭戴王冠的兔子，

以及一群兔子僕人們，

向前歡迎我們的到來。

환영 인사

은하수 다리를 건너

드디어 달에 도착했어요.

긴 망토와 왕관을 쓴 토끼와 일꾼 토끼들이

마중 나와 우리를 환영해주었어요.

Invitation from the Moon #4

A Greeting

We cross the Milky Way bridge and finally reach the Moon.

A crowned rabbit in a long cloak and its servants come out to greet us.

星光煙火

兔子們端出剛做好的年糕和散發清香的茶，

與我們共度喫茶時光。

牠們說，想和我們分享一幅壯麗的風景，

因此招待我們前來。

我們欣賞著點綴天空的星光煙火，

愉快地談天說地，直到夜深。

별꽃놀이

토끼들은 갓 지은 떡과 향긋한 차를 내와

우리와 함께 티타임을 가졌어요.

멋진 풍경을 보여주고 싶어 우리를 초대했대요.

하늘 위를 수놓는 별꽃놀이를 보며

밤이 깊도록 즐거운 대화를 이어나갔답니다.

Invitation from the Moon #5

Fireworks of Stars

The rabbits serve us fresh rice cakes and fragrant tea, and join us in tea time.
They invited us to share a great view, they say. We kept chatting deep into the
night looking at the fireworks of stars that embroidering across the sky.

夢之海

夜晚，我跌入了夢境，甚至沒有察覺何時睡著了。

星光撒落在黑藍色的夜之海上，

而我，是一名安靜划槳的航行者。

我不知道自己置身何處，又將往哪兒去，

只是無止盡地，在充滿星光的海洋中航行，

明知這是一場夢境，卻又再次地，做了一個入睡的夢。

꿈의 바다

언제 잠이 들었는지도 모르게 꿈속에 빠져든 밤.

나는 검푸른 밤바다 위 흩뿌려진 별빛 속을

조용히 노를 저어 떠나는 항해자였습니다.

지금 어디에 있는지, 어디로 가는지도 모른 채

별이 가득한 바다를 하염없이 항해하다가

꿈속이란 걸 알면서도 또다시 잠에 드는

그런 꿈을 꾸었습니다.

The Ocean in a Dream

A night submerged in a dream, unaware of falling asleep.

In the starlight scattered on top of dark waters,

I was a sailor, calmly rowing across.

Oblivious of where I was, or where I was headed,

I ceaselessly sailed across an ocean full of stars.

But knowingly, I followed the dream and continued my slumber.

當 悲傷 垂掛 時

不是所有日子，都是幸福快樂的，

偶爾，也會碰上

憂鬱、悲傷、落下幾滴眼淚

與心靈受傷的日子。

儘管如此，我之所以能夠

若無其事地拭去臉頰的淚水，綻放笑顏，

是因為你露出充滿擔憂的神情，

對沉浸在悲傷中的我，伸出了溫暖的手。

슬픔이 드리울 때
언제나 행복한 날들만 있는 건 아니에요.
우울과 슬픔. 몇 방울의 눈물과 속상한 마음.
살면서 가끔씩 그런 날도 있는 거죠.

그래도 볼에 흐른 눈물을 아무렇지 않게 슥 닦고
웃어 보일 수 있는 것은
슬픔에 빠진 나에게 따뜻한 손길을 건네던
걱정스러운 얼굴을 한 당신이 있어서예요.

When Sadness Befalls

All days cannot be of happiness. Gloominess, sadness, tears, and an upset heart—you can't help but encounter days like these, too. But I'm able to wipe tears from my cheeks and show a smile because of the warm hand you lent me and the worried face you've shown me when I was sad.

你的歇腳處

感到疲累時，就到我的懷裡來吧。

偶爾，我也想成為

能讓你倚靠、喘息的

歇腳處。

너의 안식처

힘들 땐 내 품에 안겨도 좋아.

때로는 네가 기대어 쉴 수 있는

안식처가 되고 싶어.

A Shelter for You

You can enter my arms when you're troubled.

A place you can lean on and rest,

I want to be a shelter for you.

下起
花瓣雨的一天

就算花瓣凋謝了，我們也別感到悲傷。

在花兒凋零之處，

很快地，就會冒出閃閃發亮的綠葉。

꽃비 내리던 날

비록 꽃잎이 지더라도 우리 슬퍼하지 말아요.

꽃이 지고 난 자리엔

곧 반짝이는 푸르른 잎이

돋아날 테니까요.

A Day of Floral Rain

Let us not mourn the falling petals of flowers.
Where the flowers had withered,
leaves of green will shimmer
and start to bud soon.

《成為你的森林》
幕後故事

插畫家 Aeppol 訪談

1. 森林少女的故事與角色細節是如何誕生的呢？

　　我是一邊回憶兒時喜愛的童話，一邊開始創作《成為你的森林》的。我在其中賦予了日常生活經歷的事情、開心愉快的經驗以及我的想像力，打造出細膩精緻的故事。少女身穿的衣服或周圍的裝潢，主要都是我想像自己想擁有的物品所畫出來的。沒有靈感時，我會做很多資料調查，直到出現令自己滿意的物品為止，尤其是創作衣服、背包、寢具、抱枕、窗簾時，需要仔細斟酌相襯的風格與設計。

2. 您的畫風很獨特，主要是採用何種工具來畫圖呢？

　　勾勒線條是以鉛筆，著色則全部採用 Photoshop。起初雖然想全程使用電腦作業，但我仍然鍾情於具有手感的鉛筆線條。此外，因為我會持續使用已經習慣上手

的工具,所以十年來都是使用相同品牌的鉛筆與畫本。
若是弄丟了鉛筆,就會一再地購買相同的產品。

3. 您有什麼專屬的畫畫祕訣嗎?

　　就算是一天只花三十分鐘也好,騰出時間持續作畫
是很重要的。如此努力不懈下去,某一瞬間就會實力大
增。除此之外,經常將畫作展現給他人看、獲得回饋也
很重要,畢竟畫畫並不單純只是個人的興趣而已。

　　雖然我說,最好要養成持續作畫的習慣,但這對我
而言也不是件容易的事。我通常會在家中創作,注意力
無法集中時才會到咖啡廳。我會以「喝一杯咖啡畫完一
張作品」為目標,而後就會發現,原來自己在不知不覺
中完成了好幾張作品呢。我晚上需要早睡,所以晚上不
會進行創作,而是固定從上午到下午這段時間畫畫。

4. 插畫家的生活是什麼樣子？未來的夢想是什麼呢？

　　從公司離職、開始作畫之後，收入不比過去來得優渥。雖然其他人都羨慕我是自由工作者，但有時這份自由也是一項缺點，因為很容易會偷懶。而且工作和收入並不固定，所以唯有做好時間分配和金錢管理，插畫家的生活才能夠長長久久。不過，儘管有這些缺點，我仍為自己能隨心所欲地作畫而感到心滿意足。

　　未來我的夢想是，就算成為了一位老奶奶，也能像現在一樣，持續隨心所欲地作畫。

HEART

心｜視野 心視野系列 039

成為你的森林
——走進森林女孩的日常，成為你轉身的力量！
너의 숲이 되어줄게 | 애뽈의 숲소녀 일기

作　　　者	Aeppol（周昭陳）
譯　　　者	簡郁璇
總 編 輯	何玉美
責 任 編 輯	陳如翎
封 面 設 計	李涵硯
內 文 排 版	theBAND・變設計— Ada
出 版 發 行	采實文化事業股份有限公司
行 銷 企 劃	陳佩宜・馮羿勳・黃于庭
業 務 發 行	盧金城・張世明・林踏欣・林坤蓉・王貞玉
會 計 行 政	王雅蕙・李韶婉
法 律 顧 問	第一國際法律事務所　余淑杏律師
電 子 信 箱	acme@acmebook.com.tw
采 實 官 網	http://www.acmebook.com.tw
采實粉絲團	https://www.facebook.com/acmebook01/
I S B N	978-957-8950-16-0
定　　　價	350 元
初 版 一 刷	2018 年 10 月
劃 撥 帳 號	50148859
劃 撥 戶 名	采實文化事業股份有限公司
	104 台北市中山區建國北路二段 92 號 9 樓
	電話：(02)2518-5198
	傳真：(02)2518-2098

國家圖書館出版品預行編目 (CIP) 資料

成為你的森林 / Aeppol 作；簡郁璇譯 .
-- 初版 . -- 臺北市：采實文化, 2018.10
面；　公分 . -- (心視野系列；39)
ISBN 978-957-8950-16-0(平裝)

862.6　　　　　　　　　107000704

너의 숲이 되어줄게 | 애뽈의 숲소녀 일기
Copyright © 2017 by Aeppol (So Jin Ju)
All rights reserved.
Original Korean edition published by Bakha
Chinese(complex) Translation rights arranged with Bakha
Chinese(complex) Translation Copyright ©2018 by ACME Publishing Co., Ltd.
Through M.J. Agency, in Taipei.

采實出版集團
ACME PUBLISHING GROUP